John Scalzi

*This special signed edition is
limited to 1500 numbered copies.*

This is copy 1237 .

UNLOCKED

AN ORAL HISTORY
OF HADEN'S SYNDROME

A Novella-Length Exploration
of the World of *Lock In*

John Scalzi

. . . .

SUBTERRANEAN PRESS 2014

First Edition

ISBN
978-1-59606-683-0

Subterranean Press
PO Box 190106
Burton, MI 48519

subterraneanpress.com

For Gale and Karen Scalzi,
who helped at the start of things.

INTRODUCTION

Twenty-five years ago, doctors and hospitals were receiving their first cases of the disease that was initially misdiagnosed as a variant of the Influenza A virus subtype H5N1, and then briefly known as "The Super Bowl Flu," and "The Great Flu," and then finally, after the full extent of the damage it could cause was known, named "Haden's syndrome." The disease would claim millions of lives and sentence millions more to "Lock In," a paralysis of the body that leaves the mind fully functional.

Between that first appearance and today, our nation and the world has experienced the tragedy of the onset of the disease, the triumph of the technological and social response to its challenges, and the aftermath of both—positive and negative—on our culture and the world we live in.

This document is the result of interviews with many of the doctors, scientists, politicians, and ordinary people who were instrumental in both our understanding of Haden's syndrome and our national and global response to it. While no single document can comprehensively chronicle the effects and changes to our world that Haden's syndrome created, the goal with this document is to give those who were born after its onset—some of them now fully adults—a screenshot of how the generation before them responded to what is now considered the single greatest public health challenge the planet has experienced.

It's also to remind them that while Haden's syndrome is no longer transmitting in such vast numbers, it is still one of the planet's major ongoing health issues, with tens of thousands of new cases annually in the United States alone. Only vigilance and a respect for the disease stand between us and another epidemic.

As our nation prepares to implement the former Abrams-Kettering Bill, now the "Progress With Prosperity" law, and allows private entrepreneurship to continue the work on Haden's syndrome originally funded in the public sphere, let us remember there should always be a place for the sort of basic research and prevention that can only be done by a well-funded and citizen-focused governmental organization such as the Centers for Disease Control. The CDC is happy to have funded this oral history.

—Yvette Henry, MD, Director
The Centers for Disease Control
and Prevention

PART ONE:

OUTBREAK

· ·

Benjamin Moldanado, Former Chief Investigator, Haden's syndrome, The Centers for Disease Control and Prevention:

The first thing we have to do is to admit we blew it. We misidentified Haden's at the outset. And when we did that we gave it an extra couple of weeks to spread. And that's what killed us.

Natasha Lawrence, Investigator, Haden's syndrome, The Centers for Disease Control and Prevention:

When Haden's was first moving around in the world, we were also tracking a new and aggressive variant of H5N1 influenza: bird flu. The bird flu had come up out of south China, where it probably got its start in one of the poultry factories there. It had already killed a couple dozen people in south China and we were seeing it pop up elsewhere, including London and New York, which were the first major population centers we saw Haden's in.

Haden's "first blush" symptoms were very much like the bird flu, and a number of the people who contracted Haden's also had the H5N1 virus in them as well. You apply Occam's Razor to the problem of a person having flu-like symptoms who also has the bird flu virus in their bloodstream, and it's going to tell you that the first is the cause of the second. And in 99.9 percent of the cases, that would be exactly right. In this case it was exactly wrong.

Irving Bennett, Professor of Journalism, Columbia University:

I was a science reporter at the *New York Times* when Haden's hit. I and every other science writer at the time was told it was bird flu and were asked to remind people that this was one of those years where the government had actually gotten ahead of the virus and had adequate stocks of vaccine out there, so people should go out and get their shots. Which was fine until I started hearing from doctors that the ERs were beginning to fill up with people who had the flu who also had gotten their shots.

My first assumption was that there was something wrong with the vaccine—that either it was ineffective because of poor manufacture or graft, or that it was the vaccine itself that was giving the people the flu. Either would have been a great story. I tracked some of the vaccine that looked like it was failed back to the manufacturer, SynVaxis, in Maryland, who agreed to test the remainder of the lot. Those tests came back negative, which is to say, the vaccine was perfectly effective. By this time other vaccine makers were also testing their lots, and finding nothing wrong there, either. This is when we knew for sure something else was going on. And then Super Bowl Sunday happened.

Monique Davis, MD:

I was working the ER at Lutheran Medical Center on Super Bowl Sunday. I had traded for that day because I don't actually care about football and I could bank some favors by taking the day. I figured it would be reasonably light because the Jets were in the Super Bowl, which meant that lots of the people who would otherwise be doing the stupid things that get you sent to the emergency room would be at home in front of the TV instead.

I was partly right. The day was light on gunshots and broken bones and violent trauma, but when I started my shift, the ER was already full of flu victims, mostly older people or people who didn't care they might miss the game. When I talked to them a lot of them said they already had their flu shot for the year. When I sent in the blood work I told the lab to be looking for something other than the bird flu we knew was going around.

By the time the game started the ER was packed. I texted a friend of mine over at Maimonides and he said he was getting the same thing in their ER. All over the city ERs were piling up with flu victims. Some of them were saying they tried waiting until after the game was done before they headed over but they just couldn't wait anymore. This suggested to me that when the game was done we were going to get slammed. I told the chief resident that if I were him I would get some more staff into the ER as soon as possible.

We didn't even have until the end of the game. The Jets were down thirty-five points by halftime and by the third quarter there was hardly any room to move in the ER.

Benjamin Moldanado:

New York got the worst of it on Super Bowl Sunday but we saw a sharp rise in flu-related ER visits in nearly every major US city that day. That told us that whatever we were looking at probably got into the US through New York and then dispersed through air travel. Which meant that it was easily communicable but possibly not immediately evident. People who are ill enough to need an ER aren't going to get on a plane. It was something that probably had a considerable incubation period.

Irving Bennett:

Once we figured out that it wasn't the bird flu but was another sort of flu entirely, I started looking at where it was popping up, not just in the US but elsewhere. Outside of New York, the largest pocket of "Super Bowl Flu" was London. I dug into it more and as a couple of days went on I stumbled onto an interesting bit of data, which was outside major population centers, the places that had the highest initial rate of infection for Super Bowl Flu were towns with research universities in them.

A little more digging and I discovered that on the third weekend in January the International Epidemiological Conference held its winter meeting in London and that the attendees to the winter meeting mapped really well with which university towns had the highest rates of infection. The irony of a meeting of epidemiologists being ground zero for a highly virulent new form of flu was not lost on me, or anyone else, for that matter, once the news got out.

Thomas Stevenson, former Director, National Security Agency:

When it became clear to us that the IEC winter meeting had been the likely ground zero for what we'd eventually call Haden's syndrome, we naturally began to research, within the confines of the law and always with the highest possible standard of transparency, the attendees of the winter meeting, including their recent research. We wanted to find out who might have been working on research in line with what we were seeing with the new virus. We were naturally concerned that the virus might not have occurred naturally, and that it had been designed as a potential weapon.

Was there ever a determination?

Neither we nor any other US government agency were able to officially determine the initial source of the Haden's virus, nor were we able to determine whether the virus was naturally occurring or had been genetically designed.

What about unofficially?

Quite obviously I can't comment on any unofficial findings.

Irving Bennett:

I know of two rumors that are given the most credence in the world of Haden's historians. The first is that after the First Lady came down with the disease that would eventually be named for her, a factory outside of Miranshah was airbombed into rubble. Officially the factory made cold medicines. I suppose you can guess what the unofficial suspicion was. The *Times* stringers in the area confirmed the place had been turned to rubble but neither the Pakistani nor the US government confirmed an airstrike. The official cause for the factory going up was "inter-tribal conflicts." Presumably one tribal chieftain ordered a truck filled with explosives to drive up to a loading dock and then detonate. There was a Pashtun epidemiologist at the IEC, although he was never charged with anything.

The second rumor involves a Swiss biology graduate student who had a bad breakup with his lover, a grad student in epidemiology, and also access to viral material and a gene synthesizer. Whether this dumb bastard intended for his new bug to get out into the general population is up for debate. This is a rumor because there's no hard evidence that the presumed creator of the virus did the deed, and we can't ask him because shortly after the first fatalities associated with the virus started cropping up, he took a rifle and shot the back of his head out with it. His former lover, incidentally, was fine. Never even got sick.

Both of these rumors are reasonably plausible but for practical purposes they both can't be true, so which of these two rumors you find more compelling is a personality test, in a way.

Natasha Lawrence:

It was clear this wasn't the H5N1 variant so we started breaking it down to see what we had. What we had was a virus that had a widely variable but long incubation period—that's the time between when you get the virus and when you start showing symptoms—but a short latency period, meaning the time between when you catch the virus and can start spreading it to other people. Long incubation plus short latency means there's a fairly large window for subclinical infection—people infecting each other before they feel sick themselves.

So that's what happened here. The Haden's virus is transmissible by air, which makes it easy to catch. By the time the International Epidemiological Conference winter meeting had adjourned, roughly eighty percent of the thousand or so attendees had been infected. They had been in close contact and breathing in each other's air the entire three days. And then when they dispersed they traveled back to several hundred points of origin on six separate continents, traveling in airplanes packed with other people. From a virus' point of view, you couldn't have asked for a more optimal transmission pattern.

Now, that's optimal for the virus. It's not optimal for us. When it came to the Haden's virus, by the time we knew what we were dealing with, we also knew that it had potentially already spread to millions and possibly billions of people. What we didn't know was how serious this new virus would be. We had half of New York throwing up in ER rooms, but we didn't know how long it would take for the virus to resolve itself, and for the body's own systems to beat it.

We did know we didn't have a vaccine. The Haden's virus initially presented like an influenza virus, but when we started looking at it we realized we really were looking at something new, so the sort of antivirals we use for flu—the neuraminidase and M2 inhibitors—weren't necessarily going to have the same effect on Haden's.

So no matter what, we were in for a rough time.

Monique Davis:

The first phase of Haden's looked like flu and acted like flu, but it was the worst flu we'd seen. Lots of vomiting. Lots of respiratory congestion. Fevers as people's immune responses kicked into overdrive trying to kill the virus from the inside. We treated what we could treat but after Super Bowl Sunday we knew we were up against something different.

People started to die. Old people, people with weakened immune systems. Then infants, which was heartbreaking. Those were the most vulnerable populations with any influenza infection, however, so no matter how heartbreaking, it was still understandable and to some extent expected. But then otherwise healthy people started dying as the Haden's virus just overwhelmed their systems. One kid came into the ER complaining that being sick was messing with his training for the Mohawk marathon in Albany, which was going to be run a couple of weeks later. He was dead by morning.

That was the frustrating thing about Haden's. Outside the usual at-risk groups for opportunistic viral infections there wasn't any rhyme or reason to who got sick, who got better and who didn't. It was like flipping a coin. Heads, you were sick for a day or two and then you were fine. Tails, you were laid up in the hospital for a week. Or you were dead.

About a week into it everyone stopped calling it the "Super Bowl Flu" and started calling it "The Great Flu," because it was something that just wasn't stopping. It was like the Spanish Flu in the early 20th century, except so much faster and so much more.

Benjamin Moldanado:

The parallel with the flu pandemic of 1918–20 was obvious but it's also inadequate. The Spanish Flu took two years to circle the globe because transportation was slow, and the outbreak happened at a time when the global population was under two billion. There were more than seven billion people on the planet when Haden's hit, in an era when you can get from one side of the planet to the other in less than a day. The spread of Haden's was exponentially faster and affected an exponentially larger number of people.

We did have better understanding of disease and a more coordinated global response working for us, but unfortunately given the specific nature of how the Haden's virus transmitted, those came into play only after the virus had already spread itself across the planet.

Irving Bennett:

We were having a newsroom meeting about how to deal with the coverage and my then-editor Brenda Strong said, "it's like a coordinated attack. It's like this virus has blitzkrieged every single place people live." And that's exactly what it was like. We were getting the same news reports that everyone else was seeing and it was astounding. It was literally everywhere. The only place it seemed not to be was the science stations of Antarctica. New Zealand actually stopped flights down to the South Pole to keep it from getting there.

The Haden's virus went from not even existing to becoming the major global health crisis of the 21st century in under two weeks.

Nothing like that sort of epidemic spread had ever happened before in the history of the world. It was like viruses declared war on humans and were planning to wipe us out before we could mount a counteroffensive.

Thomas Stevenson:

Before we learned of the International Epidemiologist Conference's winter meeting, we very seriously considered whether this was in fact an attack on the United States by a hostile party, either a nation state or a terrorist group. The problem was none of our chatter had indicated that something like this was in the offing, and this is, to be blunt, one of the things we had tuned ourselves to be looking for. It seemed unlikely to us that something of this scale could have been planned without our hearing of it. The enemies of the United States have a tendency to try to pump themselves up before an attempted attack. We didn't pick up any gloating transmissions before Haden's got onto our radar.

Even if Haden's had been designed to attack the US, it was a very poor instrument for the task. We were hard hit by Haden's first wave, but we and most other western and industrialized countries immediately coordinated our responses and locked down further immediate spread of the disease. It was the places without the ability to effect a coordinated response where the disease really took a bite, both immediately and with the later stages.

This is why, on a personal note, I think biological warfare ultimately never caught on. Attempting to use a biological agent against your enemy while avoiding its effects on you is like trying to use a grenade by holding onto it and hoping all the shrapnel flies in the direction of the person you want to kill. You have to be stupid or suicidal to use biological weapons. Whoever invented Haden's—if it was invented—was probably both.

Benjamin Moldanado:

Two weeks after Super Bowl Sunday we had a billion people infected worldwide, including fifty million in the United States—roughly one in seven people in both cases. By the end of four weeks it was two billion and eighty million. By the end of the year, 2.75 billion worldwide, ninety-five million in the US. One in three people across the planet got sick. 400 million died—one in every eighteen, just about.

Natasha Lawrence:

The irony today, if you want to call it that, is that people have almost forgotten just how genuinely terrifying that first stage of Haden's was. Almost four million people died in the US alone, mostly in those first couple of months. That's like wiping out the entire city of Los Angeles. In an average year, only about two and a half million people die in the US, total. We were barely equipped to deal with all the deaths, simply from the point of infrastructure.

Outside the US and industrialized nations the death toll was even higher as a percentage, and their ability to deal with the dead much lower. And that caused a huge number of problems in terms of secondary waves of disease, infection, and general political and social instability. As bad as it got for us, much of the planet had it much, much worse. There are places on the globe that still haven't entirely recovered, either in population or in terms of social structures.

Irving Bennett:

Here's an interesting fact that I learned from one of the anniversary stories coming up—it was only last year that the global population passed what it was when Haden's first struck. They used to think we'd be at something over eight and a half billion people by now.

We're a billion and a quarter people short. That's not just because Haden's killed 400 million people. It's that many of those 400 million were of childbearing age, and that in the aftermath of the disease, particularly in the developing world, a whole bunch more who would have been parents died in the messes that came after. There aren't that many things that have ever put that much of a divot into humanity's growth curve. The only other thing I can think of that most other people know about is the Black Death. That's pretty impressive company, if "impressive" is the right word to use here.

And even the Black Death usually only attacked each of its victims once.

Monique Davis:

After the first several days of the Super Bowl Flu we started getting some of the same patients back into the ER, only this time suffering from symptoms that resembled meningitis. After the first few, those of us on staff started looking at each other like, *you have got to be kidding me.* There was no way it could be coincidence that the same people who had been coming in for the flu were coming back with meningitis-like symptoms. The patients were different races, sexes, economic classes—the only thing they had in common was that they had the Super Bowl Flu first.

We started checking around at the other ERs to see if they had the same thing happening, and they did. Patients were coming back with what looked like meningitis. A lot of fewer of them than in the first round. Maybe one in four or five. But it was definitely a second stage of some sort. Now, it's possible for meningitis to be diagnosed as a flu. They share some initial symptoms. But for the same virus to exhibit flu-like symptoms, recede in most patients and then return like meningitis in a select few, that was new. And really sort of frightening.

Benjamin Moldanado:

One of the things that researchers don't want to admit, because it sounds more than a little bit sociopathic, is how interesting the Haden's virus was and what things we were hypothesizing in order to explain how it was doing what it was doing. With the meningitis-like symptoms we were confronted with the idea that a virus would attack a body, have the body's immune response beat it back to greater or lesser extent and then as a result *wholly reconfigure* the way it was attacking the body—but only in a small number of the infected.

Some of the early hypotheses included reactions to blood type or specific antibodies, a signal dependent on total viral load, or a response to specific environmental inputs, like temperature or air quality or even wireless signal. The last of those is an example of how just because it's a hypothesis doesn't mean it's good, or useful. The point was that we were looking for some reason for the virus to apparently mutate, and that led us to be occasionally wildly imaginative in our speculation. It was the most intriguing puzzle that most of us had worked with, and we're talking about a room full of people whose job it is to work on genetic material and other natural puzzles every day. It was fun—or as fun as anything could be up to the point when you remembered people were out there dying from the thing, and you were supposed to be putting a stop to that.

Our problem was that none of our hypotheses fit the data. There was no obvious single environmental or physical factor we could find that would precipitate the change we saw in the virus. At least not in the short term. This was a problem because everyone wanted to know what they could do to counteract or at least avoid the second phase of the virus attack. And we had nothing to tell them. The only way you'd know whether or not you'd get the second phase of the attack was the headache, the stiff neck, and the other symptoms. You got it or you didn't.

This was widely considered an unhelpful response from the CDC researchers, and I don't disagree with that. We were some of the smartest scientists, geneticists, and virologists in the world. We were working as hard as we could on the problem. And it seemed like the problem was working equally hard to elude us.

Natasha Lawrence:

The meningitis phase affected substantially fewer people than the flu phase but the mortality rate was substantially higher. About a quarter of the deaths associated with Haden's came from people who died in the second phase. That's because the phase didn't just present meningitis-like symptoms. The virus invaded deep into the brain and started altering brain structure in significant ways. It was literally making the brain rewire its own connections. That was another thing we didn't know a virus could really do.

In the lab we would talk about this virus like it was an evil genius. Like it was a Bond villain. It was a joke, and a way to have a little bit of levity in an otherwise depressing race against time. But in some ways it wasn't a joke at all. I think the general thought around the CDC was that this virus was actually the closest thing to malicious that a virus could get.

Monique Davis:

You could see how the second phase of the virus was working in our patients, the ones that were conscious, anyway. It would be like a series of little strokes. A little aphasia here, some loss of hearing or sight there, someone having a bit of Bell's palsy over on the next bed. Sometimes the patient would snap back immediately—the brain rewiring itself on the fly, I guess—and sometimes they'd just get worse. Some of them didn't progress, they just died. I had one patient stop talking to me mid-sentence. It took me a minute to realize she had passed. I honestly thought she had paused to collect her thoughts.

With the meningitis phase a lot of what we were doing, to be entirely upfront about it, was keeping the patients as comfortable as we could while we waited out whatever the virus was doing to their brain. A lot of people we couldn't help, and their bodies just sort of let go. Most survived and most of them seemed to recover all right, with lesser or greater short-term cognitive shortfalls that were eventually addressed with therapies similar to what stroke victims get after an incident. Some experienced permanent brain damage, again to a greater or lesser extent—there was no way to tell how bad it was going to be until it was over.

And then there were the people who experienced Lock In.

PART TWO:

HADEN'S SYNDROME

....

Neal Joseph, Biographer and Author of "The President's Crucible: The First Year of Haden's Syndrome":

I talked to David Haden, President Haden's younger brother, and the thing he told me that stuck in my head was that the President absolutely hated when the disease started being called "Haden's syndrome." Absolutely *hated* it. David said, and I remember this clearly, that it was, "Not because it reminded everyone that he was President when it hit. It was because it was named for Margie. He hated that from the minute it stuck until the end of time, everyone would think of Margie as being sick. Of being trapped in her own self. As being the person you thought of, when you thought of Haden's syndrome. Ben married this wonderful, physical, healthy, gorgeous woman and no one but him would ever think of her that way again."

Janis Massey, Chief of Staff for Margaret Haden, First Lady of the United States of America:

After Margie got sick we looked at her schedule to see when it might have happened, when that first contact with the virus might have been. After ten minutes we threw up our hands. The First Lady's schedule for the couple of weeks before she got sick had her at six events a day across five time zones in two different countries. One of those days she came into contact with school children, hospital patients, and the Prime Minister of Canada within six hours of each other. The only people who come into contact with more people on a daily basis than the First Lady are toll booth operators.

She could have gotten it from any of the people she met. She could have gotten it from us, her staff; some of us got sick around the same time and at one point half of us were out of the office with it. She could have gotten it from Ben's staff, many of whom also got sick. It was impossible to pinpoint. Which makes Margie like nearly everyone else who got sick with the virus.

Col. Lydia Harvey, MD (Ret.), Physician to the President:

The First Lady came to see me on the afternoon of the 13th, after a staff meeting, and said she was feeling achy and wanted to know if I could do anything about it. As I examined her we talked about our upcoming plans for Valentine's Day—well, she talked about hers and I admitted I had no plans because my husband was as romantic as a fish, and I'm really not much better. She laughed and said the President was the same way, but she liked an excuse to have a nice dinner for just the two of them.

By this time I was obviously aware of what was then still called the Super Bowl Flu—the President had been briefed on it by the CDC and I had been allowed to sit in on the briefing because of my position as presidential physician. But the presentation initially seemed much more like the bird flu variant that had been present at the time, and I knew that the First Lady had missed her flu vaccination—an oversight on the part of my staff. I told her it was likely to be that, though it might be the Super Bowl Flu instead, and that in either case she should consider canceling her schedule for the next couple of days and resting. She agreed to reduce her schedule for the next day but was adamant about her dinner date with the President. I told her that would probably be fine.

Elizabeth Torres, Personal Assistant to the First Lady:

The First Lady was under the weather for Valentine's Day and for a few days afterward but it didn't seem like whatever flu she had was getting the better of her. She trimmed down her schedule mostly to planning sessions with the staff, made only a few unavoidable personal appearances and kept herself hydrated. She was sick but it was a highly functional sick, if you know what I mean.

At the end of the week she decided that she was feeling better and that she could do a full weekend schedule. This included the Maryland Winter Girl Scout Jamboree, where she was going to give a speech at the closing ceremonies. She had been a Girl Scout herself, so this was something she didn't want to miss if she could avoid it.

Saturday she was fine. If she was feeling poorly she kept it to herself. She spent the morning using the White House studio for radio interviews and then had personal time for the rest of the day. When I left she seemed good. No more or less tired than she might have otherwise been. I assumed that she was over the flu.

Sunday morning she said she felt stiff and had a headache, but she said she thought it was probably due to a large margarita she had while she was binge watching old episodes of *Orange is the New Black* and then sleeping poorly. I suggested she might want to see the doctor on staff that morning, but she waved me off and took Tylenol instead and then we headed off to the Jamboree.

Ann Watson, former Reporter, WHAG-TV:

I was supposed to get three minutes with the First Lady before she went up and gave her speech, but when we arrived we were told by her press secretary Jean Allison that she wasn't going to give any pre-speech interviews. Well, I was more than a little annoyed by this. The only reason we were at the Jamboree at all was because we were promised face time, otherwise we would have just had a cameraman do crowd shots for the last two minutes of the 6:30 broadcast. I told Jean that, and reminded her that it was her office who set up the interview, not us. She apologized and kind of ducked in toward me and said, "Look, she's really not feeling well and we're just trying to get her through this thing," and that she would make it up to me. Then she walked off.

As she's saying this I can see the First Lady greeting some of the Girl Scouts. Margie Haden was very good at the public appearance face—the look of being interested or excited about something even if you don't care—and she was doing her best to use it. But you could see it slip the second she lost focus. I can't say she looked like she was in pain, but I can say that she looked very, very unhappy.

Elizabeth Torres:

By the time we arrived to the campground she said her headache had become a migraine. I was worried because as long as I knew the First Lady she had never gotten a headache that would qualify as a migraine. I asked her if she wanted to back out but she said no, she could get through it. Celia Williams and Davis Armstrong, who were in charge of her security detail, also suggested that she cancel or at the very least limit her public time at the event. She didn't want to do that. She didn't want to disappoint the scouts.

Ann Watson:

About a half hour before the closing ceremonies were supposed to start, the organizers started trying to herd all the Girl Scouts into the bleachers. They were being told that the First Lady had had something come up and she would have to give her speech early. I could hear the youngest Girl Scouts complain, because they were there for the other activities. They hardly knew who the First Lady was at all. But they were all pushed along to the bleachers.

We set up at the front with the other media and had to do a little elbow throwing because we're a small market crew, but got a good spot. Off to the side we could see the First Lady, in her winter coat, conferring with a young lady I think was her assistant and with what were obviously her Secret Service people. By now the First Lady's public appearance face was long gone. But she wasn't on stage so it probably isn't fair to note that.

She was introduced very briefly by the head scout, I think, and then she came on. The Girl Scouts started cheering and screaming for her, and if you look at the video feed and know the context, you can tell for her it was like being stabbed in the eardrums. But she smiled and waved and got out her notes and talked like a trouper for five minutes. Then she stopped, smiled and looked off stage.

Elizabeth Torres:

She looked over directly to me, said, "I think I may be having a stroke," and collapsed.

Ann Watson:

I don't think I have ever seen people move as fast as I saw those Secret Service people move when she hit the floor up there.

Col. Lydia Harvey:

When I learned that the First Lady collapsed in Maryland, after having been sick and without a member of my staff being present, I, after an appropriate time, tendered my resignation to the President. He refused it, on the basis that the First Lady did not check in with the staff to let us know she was feeling poorly. Nevertheless, it was made clear to me immediately afterwards that the refusal came counter to the suggestion of some of the top members of his team.

They had questioned my treatment of the First Lady's earlier phase of the disease and blamed me for her progressing to the second, meningitis-like phase.

Of course we know now that there was nothing that I or any physician could have done that could have changed the progression of the disease. But this is the wife of the President we're discussing. As ridiculous as it sounds, within the White House itself, it became political, quickly.

In any event, within minutes of her collapse she was on her way to Walter Reed, and so was I.

Wesley Auchincloss, Deputy Chief of Staff for President Haden:

The President was in Arizona for a meeting with western governors when he'd gotten word his wife had collapsed. They were discussing the border wall with Mexico when [Presidential Assistant] Clay Strickland leaned in and told him. The President stood up immediately and started to exit the room. The governor of Texas, who had been a primary opponent of his, started to complain, and the President held up his hand and said, "Bill, at this very moment, I could not give a single god damn for your miserable wall," and walked out. I'm certain the governor of Texas never forgave the President for that comment. I am equally certain the President did not, as he put it, give a single god damn about that.

Neal Joseph:

What was really underappreciated at the time—even after that bruising election cycle—was how much Benjamin Haden relied on Margie Haden. Much was made of the closeness of their relationship, and how it humanized him despite him being a generally unlovable character. But most people missed just how deeply he needed her, both politically and emotionally. He wouldn't have made it into the White House without her, simply put. And when she collapsed and it looked like she might have had a serious stroke, you could not have more effectively pulled the rug out from under the man than that. People were surprised that he literally put everything on pause to get back to her. They shouldn't have been surprised. It would have been surprising if he hadn't.

Col. Lydia Harvey:

The President's face when he got to Walter Reed and saw his wife in the hospital bed. You would have thought someone had torn out his heart and stamped it into the floor.

Benjamin Moldanado:

Around the time the First Lady was struck with the meningitis phase, some of the phase's earliest victims were moving into what we began to recognize as a third, distinct phase of the disease. In this phase, for all intents and purposes, the victim's voluntary nervous system shuts down—the victim can't move, can't speak, can't even blink intentionally. The autonomic systems in most cases continued to function, so people could still breathe, and all the other critical life functions would continue more or less as they normally would. Cognitive function was likewise unaffected, to the extent that it had not been earlier affected by meningitis.

The short form of this was that people suffering from the third stage were essentially trapped inside their own bodies. They were conscious, awake and able to think, feel, and perceive the world around them. They just weren't able to tell us they could do all these things. They were locked in.

At first, we only had a few reports of "lock in," and we thought it might be the rare but not entirely surprising end game for a small handful of meningitis-phase sufferers, the next step beyond those who had developed significant cognitive impairment from the disease. But then the number exploded, and we realized that many of those who were experiencing lock in weren't otherwise cognitively impaired—that there was no real correlation between cognitive damage and lock in. Like the first two rounds, some people got it and some people didn't.

And one of those who got it was Margaret Haden.

Duane Holmes, Legislative Aide for Lynn Cortez, Speaker of the House:

Nothing got done. I mean *nothing*. To be fair to the President, very little was getting done anyway: The Republicans had the Senate and we had the House and neither chamber was passing much of anything that would get past the other. But each of us had our legislative agendas, and of course the President had his own, largely in line with the Senate's. So we were all keeping busy.

Then the First Lady got sick and the President dropped everything. It wasn't subtle, either. My boss got called into a meeting by [White House Chief of Staff Kenny] Lamb, who told her that until Margie Haden got better the President's attention was going to be elsewhere. This didn't sit well with the Speaker, because we were in the middle of trying to hammer out a long-term budget deal instead of doling out extensions like we had been doing. But Lamb made it clear the President had other things on his mind. My boss said that if he was going to be that distracted maybe he should let Vice President Hicks take over as acting executive in chief. I don't think that went over particularly well.

My boss was irritated enough to ready a few jabs at the President about it, but [Senate Minority Leader Gordon] Harmon and his people pointed out to her that trying to take a punch at a man whose wife was gravely ill was not going to go over well at all. The Speaker agreed that she would give him a week but that was it. Sick wife or not, she had budget priorities, and she didn't want to lose momentum on the discussion.

As it turned out, a week later two of the Speaker's granddaughters were sick and she didn't give a crap about the budget either. Nor did anyone else—there wasn't a Congressperson on the Hill who didn't have family or friends who were sick. This plague hit everyone.

Phyllida Yang, Professor of Pathology, New York University:

Haden's syndrome really was a universal disease, and that's something that's more unusual than you might think. Part of this was that the initial vectors of infection were mobile, relatively high-status individuals: those epidemiologists who traveled across continents and came home to hospitals and universities, infecting as they went. The infection traveled as easily upward, in terms of social and economic classes, as it traveled downward. It wasn't an outbreak focused on one particular group, as, for example, AIDS was initially in the US, when it first spread among urban gay men, or as modern-day outbreaks of communicable diseases are among upper-middle-class children whose parents refuse to have them vaccinated. It went far and wide.

One consequence of this was that when it struck, there was a considerable knock-on effect because it was so widespread. Medical resources were overwhelmed, of course, but that was only the most obvious effect. Businesses came to a standstill not just because people called in sick but because spouses and parents stayed home to tend to the afflicted. Enough truckers got sick that perishable goods went bad waiting for someone to deliver them. Nearly every corner of American life was touched—and usually brought to a halt—by the initial outbreak of the disease. And as bad as it was here it was often worse in other countries, many of which did not have the infrastructure the US had built up over the years.

The one silver lining, if you want to call it that, of this universality of illness was that because everyone was either sick or knew intimately someone who was sick, there was immense political will for both short- and long-term solutions to the problems Haden's presented. And in terms of political impetus to find solutions, no one was more motivated than the President himself.

Wesley Auchincloss:

After three weeks it was clear that Margie wasn't coming out of it. Doctors elsewhere were reporting other patients by the thousands with the same issues she had, so we knew that what was happening to her wasn't isolated or unusual. And it wasn't something we could keep hidden from the press or the American people, either. It was around this time that the term "Haden's syndrome" started to be used in reference to the disease, particularly the third stage of it. We tried to keep that from the President as long as we could, but that was a futile gesture. He heard it.

Dr. Harvey and her staff confirmed by MRIs and other tests that Margie was awake and conscious, so the President spent much of his time with her at Walter Reed, talking to her and reading those mystery novels she had as her guilty pleasure. Kenny Lamb finally had to pull him aside and tell him that despite his personal pain, the country needed a president, and that President needed to be seen leading and reassuring the country in this moment of crisis. When Kenny said this, the President gave him a look that, if I had to guess, communicated supreme apathy about the needs of the rest of the country. But after a minute he nodded slowly and told Kenny that the next morning he'd be ready to resume full activity as President.

Col. Lydia Harvey:

I remember that the President stayed up with the First Lady that entire night. I suggested to him that both he and the First Lady needed their rest, but he said, more politely than I suspect he really wished to, that he was the President and that no one could stop him from speaking to his wife. I told the medical staff to give him and the First Lady privacy and to intrude only if absolutely necessary.

Nevertheless around midnight I came into the room just before heading home myself. The President was sitting on his wife's bed, facing away from me, holding her hand. I could hear him talking to her quietly. Most of it I couldn't make out, but once or twice I heard him say, "Tell me what I should do. Tell me what I need to do, Margie. Tell me."

It was a strangely intimate moment and I felt that I had intruded on something that the President did not intend nor would want me to see. I slipped out of the room before he could notice I was there, waited a moment and then knocked on the door before entering a second time, to give the President time to prepare himself. The Secret Service agents guarding the door gave me a look when I did this but as far as I know they kept quiet about it, too. I think they understood what had happened.

Wesley Auchincloss:

Kenny and I came into the Oval Office at 8AM the next morning and were surprised that the President already had the Vice President, the Secretary of State, the Secretary of Health and Human Services, the Speaker of the House, and the Majority Leader of the Senate in there with him. We had been under the impression that the meeting would be the usual agenda setter between me, Kenny, and the President. The looks we got from every other member of the meeting suggested to us that they were at least as surprised to be at the meeting as we were. We found out after the meeting that the President called each of them personally at around 5AM and told them to be in the Oval Office or face the consequences, "the consequences" being unspecified but dire. He didn't call me or Kenny, I suppose, because he knew we were coming anyway.

When we were all there, the President looked at each of us and said something along the lines of, I'll make this simple. We're going to find out what this disease is, we're going to cure it and we're going to help the people who are locked in their bodies find a way to get out, because we're the greatest nation in the world, and if we could build the atom bomb and put a man on the moon, we sure as hell can do this.

And then Speaker Cortez said, in that way of hers, "Well, Mr. President, that's going to cost money." The President said that he didn't care. [Senate Majority Leader] Caleb Waters reminded him that he'd been elected on a platform of slashing taxes and cutting government expenditures. The President stared straight at Waters and said, and this a direct quote, "That was then." Waters opened his mouth to say something else and the President said to him that he needed to listen very carefully, this was going to happen and that if anyone got in the way of it happening, regardless of party, regardless of position, he would screw them into the ground so hard that they would end up ass-first in China.

Which would have been an amusing way of putting it except that I have never, not before or since, seen the President as deadly serious as he was being at that exact moment. Waters shut his mouth and waited for what the President had to say next.

And what he said next was simple. He said to Waters and Cortez that as far as he was concerned this initiative was the sole task of the federal government from that point forward. How they wanted to get it done in their respective chambers was up to them but they had three months and no more to get a bipartisan bill on his desk, one that had more than two-thirds support in both chambers.

Left unsaid was what would happen if the bill failed to materialize in the appointed time. I think in her autobiography Cortez said she thought the President was hinting that martial law was not out of the question. There's not much that I would agree with Cortez on, politically or otherwise, but I think she was spot on with this one. To be blunt, the President was not fucking around with this one. It wasn't political, it was personal.

Duane Holmes:

It got done. It nearly killed everyone in Congress, and everyone in Congress ended up wanting to kill everyone else, but two weeks before the deadline the President had the Haden Research Initiative Act on his desk. 300 billion dollars allocated for medical and technological research and treatment for that first year, officially, and unofficially, whatever it cost to get things moving. It ended up costing three trillion dollars by the end of it. That's a hell of a lot of money.

It got done for two reasons. One, there wasn't anyone in the US who wasn't affected by the syndrome. Republican, Democrat, liberal, conservative, hippie and gun nut, atheist and evangelical, it didn't matter. Someone in your family got sick. One of your friends got sick. One of your co-workers got sick. *You* got sick.

Two, and I say this as a member of the loyal opposition, President Haden simply would not take no for an answer. He worked to pack the Congressional hearings with witnesses who would appeal on both sides of the aisle—the day [former NBA star and Basketball Hall of Famer] Marcus Shane came to testify I don't think I've seen so many grown men and women act like children scrambling for autographs. And then Shane talked about how the disease had locked in his kid and I saw [Senate Appropriation Committee Chairman] Owen Webster—that heartless bastard!—openly sobbing into his microphone. That's when any doubt I had that this thing was going to get done evaporated.

There were a few holdouts. David Abrams, who was then a back-bencher representative, made a lot of noise on the radio talk show circuit about the cost and the threat of new taxes and the expansion of big government and so on, and even took a few swipes at the President, despite them being of the same party. I understand Haden let it slide by until Abrams made a crack about the First Lady to a Tulsa talk show host. By the end of the day, as I understand it, Abrams was having a very intimate discussion with the NSA, and they showed him some pictures they had or *something*, and then that was the last anyone heard of Abrams until the act passed. He even voted for it and everything.

Thomas Stevenson:

I can't say that I have any recollection of the NSA ever meeting with David Abrams at the time. You might ask him. I would be interested in what he has to say on the matter.

Neal Joseph:

Look. At the end of the day, it came down to this: the President wanted his wife back. He was willing to do anything to make that happen. And he was President of the United States, which meant he was *able* to do anything to make it happen. As a side effect, millions would ultimately benefit from the decision, but make no mistake.

] UNLOCKED [

Benjamin Haden was being purely, entirely and unabashedly selfish. He loved his wife, he was lost without her, and he wanted her back. End of story.

Could you blame him for it? Could anyone blame him for it?

PART THREE:

THE MOON SHOT

···

Irving Bennett:

The Haden Research Initiative Act was sold to the public as a "moon shot"—as in, we went from Kennedy saying we would go to the moon to Armstrong setting foot on it in nine years because we decided as a nation that we would, and we put the resources and willpower to work. President Haden made it clear that he wanted the same unity of purpose here. And of course everyone got behind it because the syndrome touched everyone's life to a greater or lesser extent.

But it didn't change the fact that the first year of the HRIA was complete chaos. National unity of purpose is fine, but when it comes to spreading $300 billion around, logistics and a solid plan is better. And it was clear that at least at the outset, no one had a plan on how to apportion the money, to allocate resources for research and development, or to set concrete goals. The US government basically threw all that money into the air and yelled "go" to whoever grabbed it.

Haden and the rest of the government quickly realized that, and Haden in particular was incensed. He may have forced the creation of one of the biggest social programs in the history of the United States, but he still had "skinflint Republican" in his bones. The idea that his signature legislative achievement would be seen as a call to slop the pigs was something that outraged him. He sicced [Attorney General Gayle] Garcia on several companies and C-suite executives—including ones who had contributed to his election, an unheard of thing in any political era—and eventually people took the hint.

By the end of the first year things had settled out into four main buckets. One was simply for the medical maintenance of all the people who were afflicted, who weren't already covered by insurance, plus more federal backstopping for the insurance companies, who were screaming bloody murder about costs. Of the three left, one was for research into a vaccine, one for research into the brain, and the one for mobility and community research. Find a cure, communicate with the victims, get them reintegrated back into the world. It was the brain research that took off first.

Ida Garza, Former Deputy Programs Coordinator, HRIA, Department of Health and Human Services:

My job was to coordinate research across several different private companies, the CDC, and other divisions of Health and Human Services and various public and private universities, with a focus on brain research. And it was a nightmare. Primarily because each of these groups were used to shielding their intellectual property from the outside world, until such time as they could file patents or otherwise move to protect their work.

The thing with the HRIA was that as a condition of receiving funding, all the work, including work in progress, had to be submitted to a searchable database so that everyone else receiving funding could see the work and use it to advance their own work—because above anything else, we had a mandate to get advances and therapies to the patients as quickly as possible. The HRIA still allowed for patent filings, but everything, *everything*, was cross-licensed for the length of the patent, for a statutory fee that went into effect only after a product went to market.

This simply wasn't the way things had ever been done before, and so I had to deal with CEOs and chairpeople calling me up and yelling at me that they were leaving money and profits on the table. I would remind them of just how much HRIA funding they were shoveling into their companies and that they knew what the conditions were on that money. They would respond with baffled silence. Occasionally one would threaten to go over my head and talk to the Secretary, or, God forbid, the President himself.

I was secretly delighted when they would say that, because I had a standing order when that happened to refer them immediately to the White House, at which time the Chief of Staff would read them the riot act. A couple of times I understand the President himself got on the line to do the honors. I was never a huge fan of President Haden before the HRIA but I appreciated him after the fact, because he simply took no crap from anyone about how the HRIA was run. You opened up your research or you didn't participate. And there was so *much* money involved that eventually everyone gave in.

Sharing data that way was not really the optimal way of doing things. If any of us at HHS could have changed it, we would have done things Manhattan Project style, where we sent all the researchers into the desert together until they came up with things we could use. But this set-up allowed the communal effort to have at least a thin veneer of free enterprise, and that was politically important, considering the administration.

And at the end of it all, it worked. The first neural networks came about because research on detecting brain activity by way of MRI and other external devices at Stanford was combined with physical deep brain stimulation research at the Cleveland Clinic by a scientist working at General Electric. If they hadn't been able to see each other's work, they all would have had to reinvent those particular wheels. This way the wheel only had to be invented once.

Heng Chang, neural network developer, General Electric:

Before Haden's there was already a considerable amount of work being done in the field of directed brain imagery—using MRIs and other similar equipment to record and register when and how thoughts were being transmitted, and visualizing the brain as it responded to outside stimuli. At first for third-stage Haden's patients, that's how they communicated—sensors would be placed on their heads and scalps and we could very laboriously piece together their thoughts, sometimes just by running down the alphabet and having them think "yes" when we came to the letter they were thinking of. Spelling that way. Obviously that was a laborious process and not one that could be replicated for millions of Haden's patients.

When GE started researching Haden's, we got access to the HRIA database and as I was going through it I became intrigued at some experiments the Cleveland Clinic was doing with very sensitive antenna-like filaments they were developing to track incipient seizures in epilepsy patients, with the idea of then applying deep brain stimulation to arrest the seizures before they began. I thought to myself, wouldn't it be great if the filaments could send as well as receive. You could use them to allow input from outside the body directly into the brain, and sent thoughts out the same way. Then I didn't think about it again because I was working on another project entirely, and the Clinic's work wasn't on-point to that.

But my subconscious mind must have been still thinking about it because about a week later I came flying out of a dead sleep with the idea of the neural network. It was like it just downloaded directly into my brain. My reaction to it was so strong that I sat straight up in bed and actually shouted—not "Eureka!" but just a really loud gasp. This turned out not to be a great thing, because my cat was sleeping on my chest and was so surprised that she ended up digging into my skin before running off the bed. I got out of bed, swabbed the blood off my chest, and then drove to work in the middle of the night to start modeling the network I thought of. I didn't want to go back to sleep. If I did that, I was pretty sure I was going to lose it entirely.

Ida Garza:

Chang's idea was brilliant. Every scientist, on staff and off, told me so. So we knew this was a direction we needed to go, and quickly. What we didn't know was how much it would cost. There's an old saying: "Fast. Good. Cheap. Pick two." Meaning that you'd never get all three at once. We picked fast and good. We didn't assume it would be cheap, which as it turns out was a good thing.

Heng Chang:

They told me years later that by the time we got the first fully functional neural network into production, we had burned through something like a hundred billion dollars developing, testing and manufacturing it. That's a literally inconceivable amount of money to me. Certainly I never saw any of it, other than my salary at GE. But I did get on the cover of *Time* magazine and was a finalist for Person of the Year, so that made my mother proud.

Irving Bennett:

So Chang and his team developed the neural network, but one drawback they had was in its testing. They could model the networks in supercomputers which could create environments that superficially resembled the human brain, and those models got them something like eighty-five to ninety percent of the way there. But at the end of the day, if you want to find out whether they work, you have to put the networks into an actual brain.

And ultimately it has to be a human brain, for two reasons. One, because animals' brains aren't complex enough, and two, because an animal isn't going to be able to talk to you about whether the network is functioning. There was also the catch that during the meningitis phase the Haden virus changed the structure and function of the brain so much that there was literally no useful analogue in the natural world for it. If you wanted to see how the networks worked in a Haden brain, you needed an actual Haden brain.

Naturally, this created a moral and ethical issue. These first neural networks were both highly experimental and highly invasive—the work papers Chang and his crew published described how the filaments of the network would need to penetrate and migrate through the brain matter, essentially turning the brain into a massive pincushion, without any guarantee that the invasion of this artificial neural network wouldn't kill or debilitate these Haden's patients even more than they were.

When I wrote up the stories on the work papers the families of Haden's patients nearly rioted. They felt like their family members were about to be victimized a second time. President Haden had to cut short a trip to Indonesia to come back and deal with it. He was not happy about it, or with me. [*New York Times* Publisher] Bitsy Lapine called me into her office to let me know that the President had called and yelled at her about me for twenty minutes. Bitsy, bless her, eventually recited the First Amendment at him and hung up.

Heng Chang:

The media response to our initial set of work papers highlighted the problem that the public had in understanding how efficiently we could model the human brain, and the network's interaction with it. We were very comfortable that the networks could be installed safely in nearly all cases. But there was always that tiny bit of risk that you can never get rid of, and so the press and the families focused on that. There was really no way we'd be able to get volunteers from the general Haden population after that.

Irving Bennett:

This is where the near-universal nature of Haden's Syndrome came to the rescue. The first guinea pigs for the networks were eventually recruited from three distinct groups. The first was the very elderly—people who from an actuarial point of view only had a couple years of life in them even before they got sick with Haden's. The second group was people with terminal illnesses who also got Haden's—stage four cancer patients and patients with other advanced illnesses. These two groups had almost literally nothing to lose by volunteering to test these networks.

The third group—well. In one sense the people in it didn't have much to lose either. But they were still problematic, to say the least.

Chris Clarke, inmate, Nebraska State Penitentiary:

I was in prison because a couple of teenagers got into the drug lab me and my stepfather Bill had in a tool shed on our property. I think they heard from someone who bought from us that we kept our inventory there. We didn't—once we cooked it, we moved it. But they broke in, started looking around and we think accidentally started a fire. The shed went up, taking them with it. Me and Bill were charged with two counts of manslaughter and a whole bunch of drug-related charges, and were found guilty. Bill died of a heart attack before he could be sentenced, and I think the judge took it out on me. I got a total of eighty-five years, and I would have to serve fifty before I could get parole. I was twenty-two when I went in. It was a life sentence on the sly.

You would think it would have been hard for Haden's to get into a prison, but no, we got it just like everyone else. We joked that someone brought it in after a conjugal visit, but it's obviously more likely that a couple of the guards brought it in from the outside world. Within a couple of weeks it seemed like half the house was sick with it. The prison only has one doctor on staff, and then some PAs and nurses. They were swamped immediately and not a lot of help was coming in. The rest of the world had it too, and helping a bunch of murderers and rapists was low on the list of everyone else's priorities.

I think I was one of about a dozen inmates who experienced lock in. I won't bore you with the details of that. I will say it's pretty much like being in solitary, every day, all the time, for the rest of your life. That should be enough to go on. I do remember one day while I was lying in the infirmary wing, where they had permanently put those of us locked in, a nurse was talking to one of the PAs and saying that she had heard that in the legislature there were some state representatives who objected to continuing medical services to those of us who were locked in. Said it was a waste of money and that in our case it was God meting out justice. I never intentionally killed anybody, but I would have gladly wrapped my hands around that asshole's neck.

One day I hear [Nebraska State Penitentiary Staff Doctor Hunter] Graves talking to someone. When you have nothing to do but lie there and hear other people talk, you get good at knowing the voices of the staff, and this was someone new. Graves told this person that I was likely the best candidate in the infirmary. I had no idea what that meant. Then this person started talking to me. She introduced herself as Dr. Constance Dennis, from the Department of Health and Human Services, and she wanted to know if I would volunteer for a medical procedure that would allow me to talk to people again and maybe even get me back on my feet. They would advance my parole date by a couple of decades for my participation. The only catch was that the procedure was highly experimental and I might die.

Well, shit, I thought, I'm already as close to dead as I was going to get. Anything was better than this, including actual death. When they put me into that MRI to scan my brain to see my response, I was shouting "Yes!" so hard in my head that I think I almost gave myself a stroke.

Kathryn Martinez, Associate Counsel, The Prison Freedom Coalition:

We fought it. Of course we fought it. Approaching people imprisoned for life or something close to it and dangling parole in front of them in exchange for being medical experiments was deeply unethical medically and extortion besides. So we fought it, and so did the ACLU and the NAACP.

And we were shut down every step of the judicial line, culminating with the absolutely disastrous *Hicks v. Copleland* ruling. Now in the United States you can completely disregard the 8th Amendment as long as you can say that prisoner participation in a quote-unquote medical trial is quote-unquote voluntary. As if prison itself isn't a system of compulsory situations, one after the other. We set back the prisoners' rights cause by a couple of decades. It's a millstone around the neck of everyone who participated.

And it's a reminder that panic—in this case about Haden's syndrome—means that justice gets compromised. The law is blind, but the people who administer it see what way the political winds are shifting all too well.

Heng Chang:

During the worst of the *Hicks v. Copleland* controversy I'd get phone calls in the middle of the night. Some of them were from people telling me that I was a monster for using prisoners, and then others telling me that if I didn't pick their brother, or father, or whoever, to take part in the trials, they would come and burn down my house. It was a nerve-wracking time, not in the least because I had almost no say on who was chosen for the trials.

I can sympathize with those who thought we were doing something monstrous with the prisoners. My wife has Japanese-American ancestry; her family tree has people in it who were interned at Tule Lake. I know mistakes can be made because people are scared. But at the same time, there were suddenly millions of Americans, and millions more around the world, trapped inside their bodies. In places where care wasn't as advanced as it was in the developed world, third stage Haden's patients were simply being left out to die, slowly starving to death. Even here in the US there were entire hospitals basically being used as storerooms for the locked in. It was an immense humanitarian crisis, on a global scale.

I don't know. Maybe we were wrong to enlist prisoners as trial subjects. It's something I don't have a good answer for, and yes, sometimes it still keeps me up at night. But on the other hand we had workable, functional neural networks, from the moment I sat up in bed to the moment we switched on the first Haden patient, in eighteen months. That is a miracle. It really is.

Kathryn Martinez:

About a third of the prisoners recruited for the trials died or suffered moderate to significant brain damage. Or I should say, the government *only in the last five years* released the data which says a third of the prisoner participants died or suffered brain damage. We have reason to believe those numbers are, shall we say, conservative.

Chris Clarke:

Well, *I* didn't die, anyway. Though I had to wait until that Supreme Court ruling came down to get to participate in the trials. I was one of the second wave of test subjects. Since I heard that a lot of the first wave died or got brain damage, I don't suppose I should complain.

So, the way it worked is that I spent a lot of time with my head in a bunch of machines that made detailed scans of my brain. MRIs, X-rays to see blood vessels that had dye in them, that sort of thing. That took months, which didn't make sense to me. I'm not Stephen Hawking. There's not that much brain to see.

Finally they decided they knew as much about my brain as they were going to find out without actually looking at it, so they took off the top part of my skull so they could observe it directly. When they did that they took a clear, sterile piece of plastic and put it where the top of my skull used to be, so they could see inside whenever they wanted. Then they took the part of my skull they sawed off and tucked it into my stomach area, so it would stay alive for when they wanted to attach it back on to my head. I could feel the thing when it was down there. It wasn't a very good feeling.

Then they decided they'd seen enough and put the top of my skull back on, after they placed the neural network in my head. They told me that the network had tendrils that would bury themselves in my brain but that I shouldn't be able to feel them, so I shouldn't worry about them. That wasn't exactly a lie. I couldn't feel the tendrils as they dug into my brain, but every once in a while it was like one of them would hit something, and I would get a huge rush of feeling or sensation. One time my field of vision went entirely green for like an hour, and another time I suddenly started smelling oranges. Another time I had about a minute where it felt like someone put a branding iron straight up my backside. It didn't last very long but when you're feeling something like that, time stretches out.

After about a week of this I guess everything was where it was going to be, and they told me they were going to turn on the network, and that if everything worked then I would be seeing through a camera they set up on a desk, and that I would be able to talk through a speaker. Then I felt something like an electric shock and I could see myself on the bed, bald, with this ugly scar across the top of my head that made me look like Frankenstein's ugly cousin. And I thought, *Jesus, I look like shit*, and suddenly I heard the words I was thinking, coming through the speaker. The network was reading my thoughts. I realized I was going to have to be careful with what I thought until I could actually control myself. And then *that* came over the speaker.

Then I started to talk to anyone who was in the room because it had been so long since I could talk to anyone about anything. I was just asking people's names and what they were wearing and about their kids and their pets—it didn't matter because I could talk again and it was the best thing in the world. After a few minutes of this I got a weird itch on my face and it took me a couple of seconds to realize that I had tears and they were just, like, pooling on my face because I was lying down and not able to wipe them away. I had to ask someone to wipe them for me.

It was amazing. The most amazing thing. It was like being born again. It was like being free.

PART FOUR:

THREEPS

....

Summer Zapata, Author, "The Silent Revolution: Technology in the Wake of Haden's Syndrome":

The development and rapid production and installation of the neural networks was obviously the first big event in the technological history of Haden's. We spent what some not incorrectly felt was an appalling amount of money, and arguably abandoned medical morality, to develop the networks, but at the end of the day it got done, the proof of concept was there and suddenly two dozen companies, some established, some start-ups, were in the neural network business.

But the neural networks were only a partial solution. The networks gave Haden's sufferers their ability to communicate again with the outside world, but their bodies still didn't work. They still couldn't move. They were still trapped. And in many ways they were still terribly isolated.

The federal government threw billions into medical research trying to get brains to talk to the voluntary nervous system, or to grow new nerve connections, but none of that was progressing at a rate that anyone was considering satisfactory. This opened the door to a left-field solution that absolutely no one saw coming.

Rebecca Warner, Chairwoman, Sebring-Warner, Inc.:

Charlie Sebring and I knew each other growing up, but not all that well, since he was a class behind me in school and we ran in different circles. I was the stereotypical student government type and he was a classic nerd. When I graduated I went to Brown and he went to Rensselaer and I didn't see him again until the summer before my senior year, when he and I both interned at GreenWave, which my father owned. I got an internship in management, while Charlie was down in engineering. Until I caught him making things in the printers, I pretty much didn't have any contact with him.

My internship was mostly just for show because I was the owner's daughter and we all know how that goes. On one hand I was irritated with this because by this time I knew I wanted to run a company, and I didn't like people thinking I wasn't a serious person. On the other hand I really wasn't a serious person at the time, and I spent most of my time planning my summer evenings. So I couldn't complain that they give me a bunch of chumpy tasks that a monkey could do.

One of the chores I had to do was to prepare a weekly efficiency report for the GreenWave's printers. GreenWave handled a lot of bespoke production jobs for design studios and small manufacturers—everyone has their own printers but they weren't designed for large-object jobs or jobs that required more than a couple of dozen copies made. GreenWave manufactured industrial-scale printers and also kept a manufacturing wing open to handle work from other companies. Our printers were good but they were finicky and prone to breaking down, so we tracked their efficiency, and every week I compiled a report for the CTO. It was dead simple, especially since each of the printers imported their data into a spreadsheet automatically. All I really had to do was press a button to print it out.

So every week I printed them out. Most weeks I didn't look at them, but one evening I was out with friends and remembered that I forgot to do the spreadsheet, and I didn't want to be known as so inept that I couldn't even do that. So I left the party early—11PM—and went back to the office to run off the report. As I was collating the paper I actually looked at the report and noticed one printer had a weird usage pattern. It usually went off-shift at 10PM, which was the end of our second shift, but every day in the last week it was active between 11PM and midnight. So I pulled up the real time monitor and saw the printer was running right at that moment. I went down to the printer floor to see what was going on and there was Charlie, printing out something that looked like a hand. He looked very surprised to see me.

Naturally, I asked him what he was doing. He said he was doing some last-minute client work, so I said, fine, so show me the work order. We didn't do anything at GreenWave without a work order. Then Charlie got a panicked look in his eye, and that's when I realized whatever he was doing, he wasn't supposed to be doing it. So I decided to get tough with him and told him that he could either tell me what he was doing, or he could tell his boss the next morning, with me providing the spreadsheet as incriminating documents.

Charlie gave in and told me he was making a prototype. Great, I said, a prototype of what? And he explained that he had been following the development of the neural networks they were making for the Haden's syndrome people, and realized that even if they got the networks to function, people would still be stuck in bodies that didn't move. He was building a machine that would integrate with the networks so that people would be able to walk and move and get out in the world.

I asked him to tell me more, and we spent the next five hours going over everything. GreenWave had access to the Haden research database because we contracted with GE for elements of their neural networks, and Charlie had been keeping up with the neural network development. A lot of research money was going into biological solutions to fixing Haden bodies but almost nothing for machine solutions—the closest thing was an old design of a scooter with a large tablet sticking up on a post. It gave minimal mobility but no ability to hold or grasp objects or interact with people in a way that didn't feel like, well, you were a scooter with a tablet on it.

What Charlie was prototyping was much better: An actual body with touch input, shaped like a human body and with all a body's capabilities. It was a robot, but instead of a robot brain, it had a human brain controlling it. It would be a new body. One that wouldn't get tired or ever get sick like the Haden's victims' own bodies would.

Charlie kept going on and I honestly didn't understand more than about twenty percent of what he was saying. But when he was done I did two things. The first thing I did was I went and put that spreadsheet through the shredder. The second thing I did was go into my dad's office the next morning and told him I wanted every penny of my trust fund right now, and if he didn't give it to me I would tell Mom about his affair. And his other affair, too.

When Dad agreed to that, I immediately rented the use of the printer Charlie had been working on. Then I marched down to the printer floor and told Charlie to quit his internship, he and I were going into business, full partners. And he did. I took a picture of the two of us right after to commemorate the moment. He looked dazed, like he just got hit by a truck.

Summer Zapata:

On paper, Charlie Sebring and Rebecca Warner didn't look they should work together at all. She was extroverted, aggressive and business-oriented, and he was classically introverted and focused on the project, almost to the exclusion of ordinary bodily functions; there's a rumor that one day Warner came into their office and poured a gallon jug of water over his head as a hint that he should go home and take a shower.

The one thing they had in common was a commitment to the vision of what they started calling "Personal Transports." Sebring saw the practical need and had enough rigor as an engineer not to let his design wander off into the thickets. If you look at his first set of prototypes they were, from a design point, ruthlessly robotic—all function and no esthetic. He wanted Haden's patients to be able to move. He didn't care what they looked like as they did.

Warner handled all the rest of it. She kept up with the business end of the Haden Research Initiative Act and worked to exploit the gaping hole where the Personal Transports would eventually go. Warner's congressman was on the HRIA budgeting committee; she flew into DC personally to lobby him to allocate funds to biological solutions to Haden paralysis, rather than mechanical solutions. She knew that if federal funding started actively moving into her field that the project she was funding out of her own trust fund was going to get swamped.

And it worked; that year's HRIA allocations were heavy on biology and very light on mechanics. It helped that several very large pharmaceutical companies were also lobbying heavily for biological solutions, of course. But Warner's personal touch didn't hurt.

Warner also handled the esthetic aspects of the Personal Transports, driving Sebring to make them as attractive as possible before they showed them to the world. She was also the one who devised the company's publicity masterstroke.

Rebecca Warner:

They call it a publicity masterstroke but what it really was, was paying attention. The two most famous Hadens in the world were, in order, Margaret Haden and Chris Shane, Marcus Shane's toddler. They were also the two most well-connected Hadens, since once the networks were approved for general use among Hadens, they were very likely going to be two of the first people fit with them. Which meant, honestly speaking, that if we wanted to show off our wares, it made sense to work with them. So I told Charlie to make two very specific prototypes: One designed specifically for Margaret Haden, and one specifically for Chris Shane. I wanted them ready for when both had their networks installed.

The first Margaret Haden prototype Charlie took things too literally and tried to make it look like Margaret Haden, including a representation of her face. It was creepy. There's a concept called "the uncanny valley," in which something that's almost but not quite human is repulsive because you're so very aware of it being fake. This was that. I pulled him away from that direction and gave him some design points. In particular I pointed him at the female android from a very old film called *Metropolis* and suggest he use that as a starting point, although he should probably dial back the overt sexuality. Margaret Haden's public image was fit and healthy, not sexpot. It took him six tries, but he got it. Chris Shane he got in one. Children are easy.

I had developed a good relationship with [Ohio District 8 US Representative] Ed Curtis, because of his position on the House HRIA committee, and I knew that he and President Haden were friendly, so I asked him to call in one favor from the President. He was skeptical but I eventually convinced him. Ed came through and Charlie and I got an audience with President Haden where we showed him photos of the personal transport and video of it in action, being remote piloted by Charlie, and told him that a prototype was ready for the First Lady, tuned to the type of neural network I knew she had in her head.

What we hoped for was that he would be interested and that we might be able to show the prototype to him, as part of a process to getting whatever approval we needed to have the First Lady to eventually use it. But after we explained the thing to him, he looked at me and Charlie and said, "Is it here?" Meaning the prototype. And it was, since we had put it in the back of a rented panel van that we drove from Ohio. So we told him so. Then he asked, "Is it ready?" Which took me a minute to realize that he was asking whether the First Lady could use it *now*. As in, that minute.

I had no idea how to answer that. I wasn't expecting that question. President Haden stopped looking at me and looked at Charlie, who, bless his clueless heart, said "It should be, sure."

Five hours later we were in the West Bedroom, where the First Lady's body and medical team were, prepping the prototype to sync with her neural network.

Janis Massey:

I thought it was a bad idea. The President's Chief of Staff thought it was a bad idea. Mario [Schmidt, Head of the Presidential Secret Service detail] nearly had a stroke trying to argue the President out of it. But the President wouldn't be talked out of it. The only person who possibly could have talked him out of it was Margie herself, but she was willing, although it seemed to me more for her husband's sake than her own.

The personal transport was wheeled in on a gurney, along with a power source on a second gurney. I asked how it was supposed to work, and Charlie Sebring said that pretty much all the First Lady had to do was connect the thing to her internal network and then it would be under her control. Mario made a final objection that the personal transport could be dangerous or introduce viruses to the First Lady's neural network. Rebecca Warner said, more than a little peremptorily, that she and Charlie Warner would be absolutely stupid to try to give a First Lady a virus in the White House, where the Secret Service could shoot them both dead at point blank range. As I said, peremptory, but she also had a point.

They got it all set up and then Charlie Sebring said to Margie that she could connect anytime she wanted. A minute later the personal transport gave a little twitch and a jerk, and then raised its hand close to its face, as if looking at it. Then it stepped out of the gurney it was on, and everyone—*everyone*—took a step back. The personal transport walked over to the mirror in the room and stood at it for a good minute, just looking. Then, in a *very* Margie Haden move, it looked over its shoulder at the President and spoke, clearly, in a voice that sounded just like Margie's always did.

Rebecca Warner:

I remember it. She said, "I look just like C3PO!" Which, once the press got hold of the comment, is how personal transports started to be called "threeps." I never liked the term but no one ever asked me for approval, so.

Janis Massey:

The President broke down. Just broke down and collapsed knees-first to the floor. Mario started toward him, but Margie said "no," and went to him, kneeling and holding him and stroking his hair, talking softly into his ear.

For a minute or two it was strange, that here was this machine, this robot, or whatever you want to call it, kneeling down and comforting the President of the United States. And then after that minute or two, it stopped being a robot and the President and became just a wife, holding her husband, telling him that she loved him.

Rebecca Warner:

It was a beautiful and unexpected moment. It really was. And because I am who I am, while I was standing there watching this gorgeous, moving moment, I had to fight not to burst out laughing. Because the one thought that was going through my head, over and over and over, was *holy shit we're going to make so much money off this.* And we did.

Irving Bennett:

I was invited to the White House press conference by [White House Press Secretary] Adrienne McLaughlin, which was unusual and which annoyed our regular White House correspondent, but when you're told you should be at a press conference by the White House, at the White House, you go.

I was there and I noticed a number of other science and technology writers and reporters from other organizations, so I thought that we might be getting one of those occasional space-related announcements, like we're going to go Mars or something, which never pans out, and especially wouldn't pan out now, because we were spending so much money on Haden's.

Then the President comes out, and I notice that for the first time in nearly two years the man actually looks happy. He's smiling, he's waving to the press corps, and he looks like he's actually slept, which is also something that hasn't happened in two years. He walks over the podium, looks at us like the cat that ate the canary, and before we can even sit back down, says, "Ladies and gentlemen, the First Lady of the United States of America."

And in walks this golden robot, who strolls over to the podium, gives the President a hug, and then stands there, hands on the podium, and says, "So, how do I look?"

It was the first time I have ever heard complete, utter, dead silence at a Presidential press conference. And then ten seconds later we were all yelling at the top of our lungs, trying to get questions in.

Rebecca Warner:

The First Lady's press conference was huge for us. That's obvious. But it was the follow-up press conference with Chris Shane two weeks later that really sealed the deal for our company. You really can't beat a child's first steps happening because of your invention for making a good impression on the public.

We filed patents immediately, and since we hadn't taken any HRIA funding, we didn't have to accept the statutory rate when other companies came to license the technology, which they did immediately. Charlie and I were billionaires by the end of the month. I bought GreenWave from my dad, finished up or bought out remaining outside contracts and then converted the building over to making personal transports. Sebring-Warner was the first to market and the biggest name in the market from then until now. I wish Charlie had stuck around for all of it.

Summer Zapata:

Charlie Sebring is probably the classic example of a personality unsuited for success. What he was interested in was the work—the design of the personal transports, not all the politics that eventually swamped the pure joy of engineering that in the few interviews he gave he said he had felt. Sebring-Warner went from being a two-person shop to the cornerstone of an emerging industry almost literally overnight. Rebecca Warner navigated it just fine—she was born to run a company.

Sebring was less fine, and everyone I spoke to who knew him said it was remarkable just how quickly the pressure of overnight success and fame got to him. Within six months of the First Lady's press conference he became something of a recluse, sending in his work by email and avoiding everyone but trusted friends. Six months after that he told Warner he wanted out and sold his interest in the company to her at a substantially discounted rate—which to be fair only meant he was a billionaire a couple of times over rather than several times over. Six months after that he took his own life because he felt hounded by family and friends who he thought were more interested in his money than him. His suicide note was five words. "I thought I was helping."

Well, he did help. But there was everything else around the helping that drove him down. The irony is that the one person who did the most to let those who were locked in free themselves from their isolation, was the one person who ended up the most isolated and alone.

PART FIVE:

THE NEW WORLD

Josefina Ross, author, "The Undiscovered Country: Hadens and Their World":

Most people don't know this, but the word "robot" comes from a 1920s play by Czech author Karel Čapek, in which humans create artificial people as workers and slaves, and eventually those slaves revolt and replace the humans as the masters of the earth. The robots in the play weren't mindless automatons, or just machines, like what we call robots today. They were artificial people with minds and ultimately desires of their own. They were, in fact, very much like how people with Haden's syndrome became, once they were outfitted with their personal transports.

And this presented the world, finally, with the "robot revolution" that it had always imagined, through science fiction and through all those films where the machines, sooner or later, tried to displace the humans. Only this robot revolution wasn't about replacing humans, it was returning humans who had been lost to their rightful places, in robot bodies. It was a peaceful robot revolution, and that was something almost no literature, from Čapek forward, had ever prepared us for.

So it's not entirely surprising that at least at first it was rough going.

Terrell Wales, Haden's syndrome patient:

You noticed the looks but at first you really didn't give a damn because, in my case, after a year trapped in my own head, I was able to walk and talk and see and touch things again. You could have made my threep look like a 200-pound sack of manure and I wouldn't give a crap, no pun intended. So, yeah, I noticed the looks, but I didn't care. I was out.

And anyway, at the start people would stare but they would smile and ask to take a picture with you, or take a picture even if they didn't ask. Because threeps were new and still a novelty. For a couple of months there it was like being a minor celebrity. Like a character actor on a TV show or something. Then after a few more months there were more threeps around and everyone got used to us. It's like, yes, you're a robot, okay, move out of the doorway so I can get into the store. Which was fine, too, because after a while being a minor celebrity is a little annoying.

I think people started to be annoyed with threeps about maybe a year or so after I got mine. Like this: You'd go out with your friends and let's say you meet at a coffee shop. Well, the coffee shop is crowded and people are looking for somewhere to sit, and they see you sitting with your friends and they think, "That thing's metal ass is taking up a chair I could use."

I remember the first time I was out with friends at a restaurant and someone asked if they could take the seat I was sitting on. I stared at her like she was asking to strangle my cat and I told her I was using it. She said to me, "But you're not really here. You shouldn't need it." I told her to fuck off. She must have complained to the manager because the next time I went there they had a sign saying that threeps had to give up their seat if asked by a human customer. Get that—a *human* customer. I left and didn't come back but soon enough it was standard practice at most places: If you were a threep, you lose the seat.

Evangeline Davies, counsel, American Civil Liberties Union:

I was just starting at the ACLU when we got the first queries from Hadens about these incidents where they were being made to give up their seats to able-bodied people, and there were even a couple of municipalities that were passing ordinances to the effect that people with personal transports were, in a sense, second-class citizens.

You would think that would be an open and shut case with regard to the Americans with Disabilities Act, but there some wrinkles we had to consider. For example, someone with a personal transport who goes to a restaurant isn't going to eat there—their body is somewhere else, being fed something else. In effect that person is a free rider, taking up space and, some shops and restaurants argued, costing them money. They argued they had a right to ask people in personal transports to free up space for paying customers.

For another thing, if the personal transport is made to stand, is the person controlling the personal transport actually inconvenienced? They aren't being physically inconvenienced, because their body isn't there. Having the personal transport stand won't tire out the person controlling it. The argument could be made—and was—that asking personal transports to stand was no more inconveniencing to them than requiring able-bodied people to wear shoes. You could argue it's humiliating to make someone stand when the rest of their party is sitting, but bars and coffee shops could point to groups of able-bodied people crowded around a single table, some standing and some sitting, and say that none of them were being humiliated. And so on.

In one sense these seem like trivial things to be worrying about or to take to court. But they were actually hugely important. Almost overnight the world had developed what really was a new nation—a group of people whose commonality of experience was unlike anything anyone had ever experienced before. There were roughly the same number of Hadens in the US as there were religious Jews. More than the number of Muslims. They experience the world in a unique way, and because of how they present to the world—either in personal transports or as online avatars—they will experience things that no other people experience in quite the same way, including violations of their rights. We and other rights organizations had an opportunity that we hadn't had before, to trim off discrimination *before* it developed. I think in the end we were more successful than we expected, but less successful than we'd hoped.

Terrell Wales:

When I was a kid I watched a documentary about the movie *Planet of the Apes*. The first one, with Charlton Heston. They were talking about how they would make up all the extras as various types of apes, like chimps and gorillas and orangutans, and then the extras would go to lunch and they would segregate. All the people made up like gorillas would sit with other gorillas, all the chimps would sit with chimps.

It started being like that with other Hadens. Whoever you were before, you started being this other person too. Someone who none of your other friends could imagine being. It wasn't their fault. They just never went through the process of being trapped in their own skull and never knowing if they would ever talk to anyone ever again. I suppose maybe it's like being in a war. You had to be there, and eventually you start spending all your time with the people who *were* there, because they knew what it was like.

I would see other threeps on the street and we would do a wireless handshake with each other where we would send each other our addresses as we walked by. Later on we would sign on into the Agora—the first version of it, the one that was like a quest-oriented video game without the quests—and find each other and just hang around and talk. On the Agora we had avatars that looked like our bodies did when we were healthy—hardly anyone faked their image at first—and you could be yourself, or something close enough to yourself that it felt normal.

I'm not sure when it was that I started thinking of myself as a "Haden." It snuck up on me. I think it started when I realized that no matter how much I tried to pretend that looking like a robot didn't mean anything, it *did* mean something, in the way people thought about me and reacted to me. Not just about whether I could take a seat at Starbucks, but whether people treated me like an actual human being. I had some drunk son of a bitch break a beer bottle over my threep's head once because he wanted to see if it would hurt me. I had to keep from breaking his nose with my metal fist, which I *knew* would hurt *him*.

I think I finally knew I was a Haden one night when I went out with a bunch of high school friends to a bar, and they were just sitting there drinking and bullshitting each other, and I was sitting and bullshitting with them, but what I was really doing was checking into the Agora and making plans with friends there to run a game with them as soon as I could get away from my meatpals—"meatpals" meaning people you knew outside the Haden world. I was doing my time with my meatpals but waiting to get back to my real world.

I had become a chimp, and wanted to go sit with the other chimps, I guess.

Josefina Ross:

One thing it would be wrong to do is to think of the Haden community as one homogenous group, just because they all had the same disease afflict them. In reality the only thing they all had in common was the disease. Otherwise, Hadens are one of the most diverse communities that ever existed. There are rich Hadens and poor Hadens, educated and ignorant Hadens, Hadens of every creed, color, gender, sexual and political orientation, age and previous health status. In the United States, at least, the Haden community was a mirror of society at large.

And because of that there were some immediate schisms in the Haden community, even as it was realizing it *was* a community. One of the largest schisms, and one that remains to this day, was the one between the Hadens who spent most of their time in the physical world, through personal transports and daily interaction with non-Haden family and friends, and the ones whose lives were inward-facing into the new world that the Hadens had started to create, through the Agora and other spaces and social structures that they'd established.

That schism was partially but not entirely predicated on age, and other factors played into it as well, like how strong the Haden's physical world support structure was, as well as certain personality markers. Hadens who were naturally introverted were slightly more likely to spend more of their time facing inward to the Haden community.

The number of Hadens who were entirely one way or another was small, of course, but the general division was real, and had a substantial impact on how the community as a whole began to define itself.

Terrell Wales:

The other thing to consider is that after a while the physical world just becomes depressing. Look, in the online Haden space, I have what you could call a house—it's a permanent chunk of a server that I own. I'm able to build and create there.

So my house is a log cabin in about six square miles of virtual Vermont forest. Even when I first got the server space the technology was good enough that you could walk right up to the trees and you could see all this detail, and all the other sensory data could be piped in. You could have every day be peak foliage season if you want to. I did that for about a year once. A creek runs out by my cabin, and I see deer and foxes walk by. It's all gorgeous. And it's all mine. And maybe it's not real, in the sense that it physically exists in the world, but you know what? I sit on my porch and look out into the woods and it feels real enough. I'm home.

And then I have to come back into the physical world. And first off, I have this bloated, pale body that doesn't move. Food comes in by a tube and then a few hours later goes out in a tube. The body—my body, *me*—sits in room piled up with medical equipment and charging chair for my threep. I share an apartment with three other Hadens, with a spare room for our caregiver. It's the world's most depressing bachelor pad. And then I go out in my threep, and I never quite forget that I look like a piece of CGI in an old science fiction movie.

I mean, you tell me. Which would you rather spend time in? That log cabin in Vermont, or the crappy apartment stuffed with dudes in tubes? Is this even a question?

Irving Bennett:

I filed a number of stories about the Haden community before we hired Tanna Hughey, who was a Haden herself and could report from the inside, as it were. In the early days, when I would give talks about covering the community, the parallel I would give people to describe Hadens was the deaf community. The deaf community is largely invisible to people who aren't in it, but on the inside it has a very strong sense of identity that's informed by the one thing they have in common: their deafness.

But within that community there have always been factions. Those who wanted their children educated in sign language versus those who wanted their children educated in English. Those who saw the benefit of cochlear implants versus those who saw them as a threat to the cohesiveness of the community. Those who wanted to spend their time in the larger culture, and those who felt it was more important to help the deaf community develop its own unique culture.

The Haden community was very much the same way—with its own unique variations and spins, of course. But what was obvious from even the early days was that there were some people who saw contracting Haden's as the worst thing that ever happened to them, and were desperately searching for a way out of it. And then there some for whom Haden's was the best thing to happen to them. Suddenly they had a community and opportunities where they might not have had them before. Their world quickly became everything inside—stepping outside of it when they had to, but only then.

For them, being a Haden was a cornerstone to their identity. Making other people understand that, Hadens and non-Hadens both, was the challenge they had to deal with. Some things were easier to deal with than others.

Lawana Dellinger, Haden's syndrome patient:

I met Michael in the Agora, at a singles' mixer. This was early, when it was still a little strange to think about dating or relationships between Hadens. Not just because of our bodies being locked up but because often you'd meet someone who was thousands of miles away. But then you'd think, well, why does it matter that we're thousands of miles away? It's not like we're going to go for long walks anyway. So we all got over it.

I liked Michael right away. He was funny and smart and we were both football fans, although I was a Giants fan and he was for the Raiders. I decided I could overlook that, and we started dating. About a year later he proposed. I said yes. My family wasn't entirely happy about it. I think my mother was under the idea that despite the fact I visited her in my threep every day, I was in a coma of some sort. So Michael was taking advantage of poor, defenseless me. My father talked her through it. We had two weddings. One at First Baptist, in our threeps, and one in the Agora with our Haden friends. We moved in together at the Haden residential wing of George Washington University Hospital.

After we'd been married for about a year, Michael and I were talking one night about the future and what we wanted to do with our lives, and I said something like, well, before I got sick I wanted to have kids, but now that's not possible—and then Michael stopped me and said, what do you mean it's not possible? And I started to say something about it and then just sort of let my mouth hang open. Because there was no reason I couldn't have children. Biologically. And there was no reason *we* couldn't have children. It would be complicated, and we definitely wouldn't be having them the old-fashioned way. But we could have them.

So we went to our doctor and said, we want to have children. She looked at us like we had turned into poodles. And finally she said, I think we need to have this cleared. And we said, why? We're adults, we're of sound mind, and my body can carry a child, can't it? We started pressing her for reasons why she seemed uncertain. The more we talked to her the more defensive she got and the angrier I got. By the time we left the office I was either going to cry or kill her.

But she was just the first. We talked to five or six doctors about it at the hospital and none of them would do it. There was no medical reason—I was a Haden but I was healthy and my reproductive system worked just fine—so there had to be some other reason for it. And of course the reason was obvious. So was what came next.

Evangeline Davies:

Dellinger v. George Washington University Hospitals was a huge case for us, in terms of advancing the rights of Hadens. It was a reminder that first of all, Hadens were still human beings, with the same rights and opportunities, and that those couldn't be taken away merely due to prejudice or statistically unwarranted concerns over liability.

It also—and importantly—forestalled a lot of other cases that we would have to take on. *Dellinger* raced through the courts and the decision at the Supreme Court was 9-0. It was a precedent you could hang your hat on. A lot of Haden-related cases we had settled out immediately afterward.

Also it was the first case I ever got to argue in front of the Supreme Court, so I have good memories there.

Lawana Dellinger:

We named our first daughter Evangeline. It was a way of saying thank you.

And yes, being Haden parents to non-Haden babies was a challenge. It's very hard to describe how strange it is to be in your threep, holding your infant steady while she nurses at your breast. And whether or not we won the court case, we still got lots of looks when we'd take Eva to the park. More than once we got asked by police to prove she was ours. It took everything I had sometimes to keep from hitting someone.

We got flack from Hadens too—I get notes saying that because our children were non-Haden, we were not committed enough to the Haden cause. And I was like, excuse me? There's a cause? Look, I'd like to help you with your cause and all, but right now I've got a diaper to clean out. My daughter takes precedence over your *cause*.

Eventually people forgot about us, which was fine. Now we have two daughters and a son, and my son likes to joke that he has two sets of parents, but one of them doesn't get out much. He thinks the joke is funnier than it is. We're a normal family, really. And I think that this tells you that even in this new world of Hadens, or however you want to put it, there's still people in it, just trying to live their lives. That's the real story of any world you live in, isn't it.

PART SIX:

TWENTY-FIVE YEARS

....

Monique Davis:

Does it feel like twenty-five years? No, but I don't think long stretches of time ever quote-unquote feel like however long they are. My daughter was born eighteen years ago. I look at her sometimes and it feels like she was a toddler yesterday. Everything in the past gets compressed together. It's compacted for easy sorting, maybe.

But every once in a while I remember how long it's been. This year's crop of internists includes a doctor who contracted Haden's in the womb. She's smart as they come, and her entire life has been spent in a threep. I think about that and I shudder; she doesn't think about it at all. It's just always how her life has been. Most of her fellow internists, none of whom remember life before Haden's, don't think it's that unusual, either. *That's* when it feels like twenty-five years.

Natasha Lawrence:

What bothers me after twenty-five years is that we still don't have an effective vaccine. We still don't have a cure. What we have are established protocols for locking down the spread of the virus when it surfaces, and a whole array of therapeutic machines to mitigate the effects of lock in. We can't stop the disease. We just make it less awful when it happens.

And yes, that feels like a failure to me. In the last two and a half decades we've learned so much about the brain. We've made enormous steps in integrating these brain prostheses and have built entire industries around serving Hadens and making their lives easier and more tolerable. And still every year hundreds of thousands of Americans get sick with the latest strain of the Haden virus. Tens of thousands die. Tens of thousands experience lock in.

You know what it's like now? It's like car accidents. Even with automated cars, people still get into car accidents, because they try to overrule their autodrive or refuse to engage it. We still lose ten to twenty thousand people a year in traffic accidents. No one thinks of it as an epidemic. It's just the cost of doing business. The cost of living our lives. Haden's syndrome has become that now. A chronic disease of our nation, and of the planet.

Thomas Stevenson:

My understanding, or at least the way it was explained to me, was that the Haden virus is simply a highly adaptable and easily mutating virus; that enough changes about it from year to year and season to season that we simply have a hard time keeping up. One of the questions I had early on was whether this high rate of mutation was something we were seeing in the lab, or whether it might be that new strains were being designed or at least cultivated elsewhere and released into the population. We did see mutation in the lab, but not at the rate we would expect for the level of mutation in the wild. As with so many things about this virus, our data was ultimately inconclusive.

Elizabeth Torres:

They didn't catch Margie Haden's cervical cancer early enough, so by the time it had been diagnosed it had metastasized, into her liver and her lungs and brain. And I remember very clearly what she said to me. She said, "This is a victory, Liz. I lived long enough to die of something else completely." And then she laughed.

I thought it was her lighting a candle rather than cursing the darkness, if you know what I mean, but that night I understood what she meant. It was a reminder that the disease that she gave her name to—the disease that defined her in ways I know she wished it hadn't—was not the only thing about her life. She lived long enough to die a "normal" death. Now, maybe that wouldn't mean anything to anyone else. But it meant something to her.

Haden's did give her one small blessing. Her personal transport allowed her to see people and be seen, right until the end. She never tried to hide what was going on with her physical body, but by then people were so used to her being in her threep that she was able to use it to say goodbye to the people who were important to her, and not trouble those who didn't want to be troubled. It made it easier for her to make it easier for others. And that was Margie all over. When we laid her down next to Ben, I knew she had come to her happy ending.

Duane Holmes:

Nothing ever gets forgotten in Washington. David Abrams never forgot getting stuffed by President Haden over the HRIA and as soon as Haden was out of office, he started trying to get it trimmed back. A program here, a research initiative there, divots to the HRIA attached as riders to farm bills. The usual things. Sometimes he'd get something defunded, sometimes he wouldn't. He was in a safe district, he could take his time about it.

By the time he switched over to the Senate, he'd gotten some real momentum behind scaling back the HRIA. He campaigned on it and he almost got the Senate behind him, but then Ben Haden died and at the funeral Margie Haden started talking about the HRIA as her husband's "enduring legacy." And that was pretty much that for Abrams' first try. It'd take him a couple more tries before he could get enough traction in the House and Senate to cut it down.

But he did. The HRIA has been replaced by "Progress With Prosperity," whatever the hell that means. Dave Abrams is enjoying his moment as the people's champion—he's lowered their taxes, which always plays, I mean, that's how Haden got elected in the first place—but I think if you got Abrams alone with three or four drinks in him, the truth would come out. He got the HRIA defunded because he hated President Haden's guts, end of story.

Rebecca Warner:

The HRIA didn't have to end, not in the stupid way it did. And it wouldn't have ended if the government would have allowed us to open sales of threeps, and other companies their neural networks, to non-Haden's syndrome patients. The argument always was that implanting neural networks was too risky for people who were not already locked in and had their brains changed by the virus, and that the HRIA could only be funded, politically, if threeps and neural networks and everything else were medical devices.

Well, I always thought it was bullshit, and I wasn't shy about saying that. We had all sorts of people wanting neural networks and threeps—people who could benefit from them. People who were neurotypical but paralyzed. Older Americans. I had eighty year olds yelling at me to give them threeps so they wouldn't be trapped in their nursing homes. And I wanted to give them threeps! But as long as we were taking the HRIA money, we had to play by their rules. Money you know you will get is worth more than the money you might get. It's that simple. But at the end of the day Hadens are still only a few million people. There's a multiple more senior citizens in the United States. Set them up with a threep as part of their Medicaid package and we'd have another boom economy overnight.

The Abrams-Kettering Bill is the worst possible way to move from federal funding to private enterprise. We have almost no time to prepare. Our customer base is stranded because the federal funds they had incorporated into their budgets aren't there anymore. We have no customer base outside the Hadens and the cost of R&D for designing products for new potential customers is going to kill us. I've never been ashamed to call myself conservative, and I don't mind having the HRIA go away. But it should have been done intelligently. You don't crater the economy just to make political points.

It's going to be a tough few years. We'll have to see what happens now.

Heng Chang:

If you ask me what the most surprising thing was in the last twenty-five years, I'd say it was our discovery that the neural nets didn't just allow Hadens the ability to use computers and body prostheses like personal transports, but that they could under very specific conditions also allow one Haden to actually overlay their consciousness on another's, in the same brain. We discovered it by accident, and it doesn't have any value for most Haden's patients since their bodies don't move. But then we discovered that a small percentage of people who recovered from the second stage of the virus had their brains changed enough to do it too.

That's how we got Integrators—the people who can carry other people around in their heads. Here in the lab the word we used to describe at the time it was "spooky." It was spooky. Even now I have a hard time imagining what it must be like to be an Integrator. I understand *how* it works, technically. But I don't *feel* it.

Terrell Wales:

This sounds funny coming from a man who spends a lot of his life inside a robot, but the moment I really knew I was living in the future was when I got a chance to use an Integrator. There aren't many of them, so the NIH puts you in a lottery and if your name comes up, you get a day. My name came up and I got ported in and then for the first time in years I was in a full-fledged, no-bullshit functioning human body.

You want to know the first thing I did? I went to the International House of Pancakes and ate so many damn pancakes and sausage links I just about made the Integrator throw up. Then I had an ice cold Pepsi. Then I had a cigarette.

Uh. I don't think I should probably say what I did after that. I'm not entirely sure it's legal.

The weird thing—well, weirder thing—is that all the time I was running around with the Integrator's body, he's in there with me. And I wondered, what the hell does this guy do when people are using his body? Doesn't he get bored? I'm pretty sure every Haden who gets to use a real live human body does what I did, which is to eat, drink, and get laid. Except for the last part, it must get monotonous. Also, because I'm sure I almost made him puke, I wondered how often that happens, right—someone pushes the Integrator's body to an extreme point.

I didn't wonder about it too much, though. I was on a clock, and I had things to do. But, yeah. Of all the things since Haden's first hit, that was the one that made me think, wow, things really are different. And weird.

] UNLOCKED [

Chris Clarke:

Well, *my* life hasn't changed a damn bit, to tell you the truth. I'm still not eligible for parole for another five years.

Irving Bennett:

When I retired from the practice of journalism and started teaching it instead, I began using Haden's syndrome as an example of the fact that sooner or later, everything simply becomes daily life. When Haden's first struck, it was the most important news story of the century. Everyone knew it. Everyone felt it. But then it just… became part of the fabric of the American story, day in and day out. Something commonplace. Something quite literally quotidian. The half-life between story of the century and not even the story of the day is quicker than you would ever guess.

But then I ask my students: does this mean that it stops being a story worth telling? And I say to them the real journalists among them know the answer even before I ask the question. And the answer is that the story is worth telling every day. The trick is not to find the story of the century. You won't miss that story when it happens. No one will miss it. The trick is to find the story of the day and *for that day* make whoever reads it or hears it care about it so intensely that it doesn't leave them. Then it becomes a story of their life. Maybe even *the* story of their life.

Some of the students look at me like I'm trying to pull a fast one on them. Others don't even care. But in every class there's one or two who get what I'm trying to tell them. They're who I'm teaching to. They're the ones who after they leave this place, are going to go out in the world, take a look at Haden's, or whatever, and discover there are still so many stories there yet to tell.

I'm looking forward to those stories.